But Not Kate

For Grandma and Grandpa

 Inquiries should be addressed to Lothrop, Lee & Shepard Books, a division of William Morrow & Company, Inc., 1350 Avenue of the Americas, New York, New York 10019. Printed in Italy.

First Edition 1 2 3 4 5 6 7 8 9 10

Library of Congress Cataloging in Publication Data
Moss, Marissa. But not Kate / by Marissa Moss.
p. cm. Summary: Kate compares herself to the other kids in school and fears that there is nothing special about her, until she becomes the magician's helper in an assembly. ISBN 0-688-10600-5. — ISBN 0-688-10601-3 (lib. bdg.) [1. Individuality—Fiction. 2. Magicians—Fiction. 3. Schools—Fiction.] I. Title. PZ7.M8535Bu 1992 [E]—dc20 90-25751 CIP AC

Marissa Moss

But Not Kate

Lothrop, Lee & Shepard Books New York

Ellen waved her baseball cap.
Ben had a great new mitt.
Sonja's shoes had polka dots.
Everyone had something special...
everyone but Kate.

Sarah wrote the neatest
and Emma raised her hand.
Peter always knew the answer,
but the teacher called on Kate.

Aa Bb Cc Dd Ee Ff Gg Hh Ii
1 x 10 = 10
2 x 10 = 20
3 x 10 =

Lee D.
shirley

Alfred drew good elephants.
Hester's cow had charm.
Christopher was best at bats.
Kate didn't know what to paint.

May ate chocolate cupcakes,
the kind with sprinkles on top.
Lucy had a quarter to buy a popsicle.
Sam had berry pie.
Kate had the same old lunch,
just an apple for dessert.

"Assembly time!" called Jeff. "I'm first in line."
Lee was second, Margo third.
Kate was last.

ASSEMBLY
TODAY
MAGIC
SHOW
2:00
line up here

The curtain parted and
Abra Shazam bowed low.
"A volunteer!" he called.

Everyone shouted, "Me! Me! Me!"
But not Kate.
Peter waved his hand high.
"Pick me! Pick me!" May cried.
Lucy begged, "Can I help, please?"

But Abra Shazam chose Kate.
"You!" he said, "You're my helper!
You look magical to me."
"Not me," Kate mumbled.
"Yes, you," said Shazam.
"Here, tap my hat with this wand."

"I can't," said Kate.
But everyone was waiting,
waiting just for Kate.

She took the wand. She tapped the hat.
Flowers filled the air.
"Magic!" Kate giggled.

"You're magic!" said Shazam.
"Now can you reach inside my hat?"
Kate pulled out a rabbit,
then another and another.
"It's magic and I did it!"
"But of course," said Shazam.

"Now for the hardest trick of all,"
announced Abra Shazam.
"The wondrous scarf of a thousand stars!
Hold this end, give it a tug, and say the magic word.
Say it loud, with all your magic,
or the trick won't work."

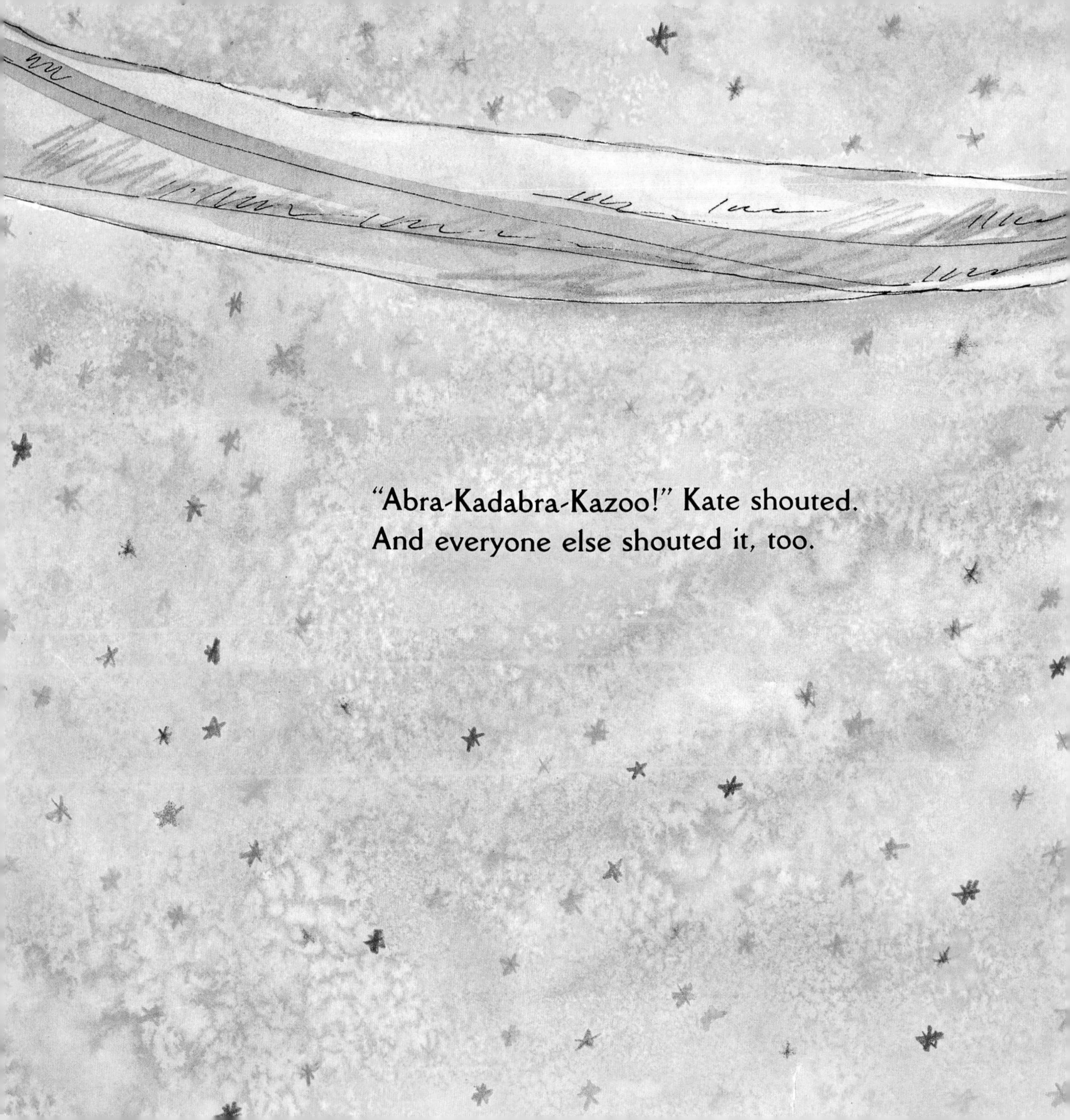

"Abra-Kadabra-Kazoo!" Kate shouted.
And everyone else shouted it, too.

"Stars!" cried Kate. "A thousand stars!"
"Your stars," said Abra Shazam.
"Keep them, my thanks to you.
And thank you everyone."

Stars glittered in their eyes.
Abra-Kadabra-Kazoo rang in their ears.
Everyone felt magical,
but no one more than Kate.